THE PORRIDGE PLOT

ALMA BOOKS LTD
3 Castle Yard
Richmond
Surrey TW10 6TF
United Kingdom
www.almajunior.com

The Porridge Plot first published by Alma Books Ltd in 2017

© Che Golden, 2017

Cover and inside illustrations © Becka Moor, 2017

Che Golden asserts her moral right to be identified as the author of this work in accordance with the Copyright, Designs and Patents Act 1988

Printed and bound by CPI Group (UK) Ltd, Croydon, CR0 4YY

ISBN: 978-1-84688-414-6

The Porridge Plot

CHE GOLDEN

ALMA BOOKS

FOR MAYA

MAY YOU ALWAYS
HAVE KETCHUP

THE PORRIDGE PLOT

CHAPTER ONE

It was a pretty house. Surrounded by a white picket fence with a gate that swung open into a small garden full of summer flowers, it was very different from the cramped flat they had left behind in the city. In their old flat, the sound of the traffic had been a constant hum, a backdrop to their lives. But all Maya Brown could hear now was the drone of a furry bumblebee, as it glided from flower to flower, and birds singing in the trees around the house. Sitting all by itself in a lush garden, it was picture-perfect. It even had a plant growing around the door that was covered in tiny, star-shaped pink flowers.

Maya hated it.

"Come on then, little squid, let me carry you over the threshold," said her father, and before she could say anything he scooped her up in his arms, kicked the gate open and walked down the garden path, bouncing her in his arms.

Maya was in no mood to be cheered up, and she scowled at her mother's laughing face over her father's shoulder, and she scowled at her brother, Liam, who scowled back, earphones firmly jammed into his ears.

Her father struggled to turn the key in a rusty-looking lock; when the door finally swung open, he said, "Welcome to your new castle, my little princess!" before sweeping Maya into the house. It was a shame he forgot the door frame was lower on the new house than it was in their old apartment block.

"*Ow!*" shrieked Maya, clutching at her forehead as the hallway spun around and stars sparked in front of her eyes.

"Would you *please* be careful," Mum scolded behind them, as Dad put her down on the ground. He bent his long legs until his brown eyes were level with her green ones.

"You OK, little squid?" he asked. "I'm so sorry, I didn't mean to hurt you."

But it did hurt, and Maya could feel hot tears building up behind her eyeballs as her forehead throbbed. Before she could burst into tears, Mum was crouching down in front of her, taking her flushed face in her hands and kissing the lump that was beginning to swell on her forehead. "There, there, darling, let Mummy kiss it better."

Liam stood over her and sighed, pulling the white plastic earphones from his ears.

"Just let her cry – it's all she ever does anyway," he sneered. "It will make the place feel more like home." He looked around the gloomy hallway. "It needs all the help it can get."

Maya gritted her teeth, darted round Mum and kicked her brother hard in the ankle. He yelled and clutched at his shin, while Maya spun round and made a run for it. "Could you not leave her alone, just for one day?" she heard her mother say to her brother, while her father chuckled and said, "There's nothing wrong with her aim."

But this wasn't home, where her feet would guide her quickly to her bedroom or the nearest small space that she could squeeze herself into and hide away from the rest of her family. She had no idea where she was going and, as she stumbled into the living room, she stopped and stared.

"Do you like it?" asked Mum.

Maya looked at the faded floral wallpaper, the dusty floorboards, the shadows that hung like cobwebs in the corners, the dirty fireplace that smelt of wet coal dust and the filthy multi-paned window, which seemed to dilute the sunlight. She looked up at her mother and shook her head. Mum sighed and held out her hand. Maya clutched at it and felt her heart lift when Mum gave her fingers a little squeeze.

"After a good scrub and with all our things in here, it will feel just like home," said Mum. "You'll see."

Maya looked around, a frown puckering her forehead. "It's dark," she said, in a voice so small it was almost a whisper.

Mum shrugged. "Older houses often are," she said. "They didn't have double glazing when these houses were built, so they didn't want to put in huge windows and let too much heat escape. But we'll take down all this dark wallpaper and paint the walls bright colours – it will make a big difference." Her eyes sparkled. "In fact, I can show you right now how good it can look. Follow me, I have a surprise for you!"

Maya took one last look around the neglected living room and then followed her mother back into the hall-way and up the narrowest staircase Maya had ever seen. It was enclosed on both sides, and she was sure Mum was having to breathe in to have enough room to move.

"Ta-da!" Mum threw open one of the wooden doors on the upstairs landing and ushered Maya into the room.

It was pink and green, her favourite colours. Billowy white curtains hung at the small window. Maya walked across the polished floorboards, her footsteps echoing in the empty room, and peered out of the window. Open fields stretched away from the garden fence. There was nothing moving in it, except for a few birds. It looked as empty as a desert to Maya.

"What do you think?" asked Mum, a big smile on her face. "I came down here on the weekend to get the room ready for you. Isn't it lovely? I tried to make it look like your old room – I know you loved it, but this one's much bigger: you have a lot more space to play here!"

Maya bit her lip as she tried to imagine her stuff in here. She had liked her tiny boxroom in their old flat. She liked the way all her cuddly toys, dolls and books had taken up every bit of wall space. When she lay in her bed, she felt cocooned by them all. Her room had been her den, the one place in their flat that didn't have two people in it all the time, because there just wasn't the space. She had liked the view from her old window better as well. She could watch all the children playing in the park opposite their block of flats, and no one even knew she was there. In her old room she could lie in her bed and listen to the babble of sounds – slightly muffled by the double glazing – that was London, plucking noises from the stream and holding each one in her mind, like a bright, shiny pebble, while she figured out what that noise was. She could take her time and do it without other children laughing at her and telling her she was stupid or adults getting frustrated.

Maya noticed that Mum was still watching her, her happy smile wavering a little. She felt guilty, realizing all the hard work Mum must have done to surprise her, and she offered her a weak little smile of her own.

Mum sighed. "I know it's a lot to get used to, but we are going to be very happy here, Maya – just give it a chance. Shall we go and give the boys a hand unloading the car?"

Maya nodded and followed Mum out of the echoey room. But as Mum started to walk down the stairs, Maya noticed a door that was narrower than the others on the landing, and it was slightly ajar, showing stairs with light filtering from above. Curious, Maya opened it and climbed stairs that were so steep it was almost like climbing a ladder – she had to use her hands on the steps above to get a secure grip. But once her head poked through the floor above, her mouth dropped open in surprise.

The attic room was huge, with deep, sloping eaves that Maya could just about stand beneath. There was a tiny little cast-iron fireplace at one end of the room and a square window set in the roof with a clear view of the sky above. It was filthy and unlived in, and the dust on the floorboards was so thick it puffed up in little clouds beneath Maya's feet as she walked across the room. Dirty cobwebs hung like rags from the beams, and the whole place smelt like old apples. She loved it.

"Maya, what are you doing up here?" asked Mum as her head appeared through the floor. She frowned when she saw how happy Maya looked. "Oh no, Maya, it's so dusty up here, and there is a lovely room waiting for you downstairs."

"Please, Mummy," said Maya, clasping her hands in front of her face. "I really, really like this room. *Pleeeeaase.*"

Mum grimaced as she tried to stand up straight under the eaves and realized she couldn't. "But it isn't really a proper room, Maya. There's no central heating up here, for a start."

Maya's face fell.

Mum sighed. "Let's see what your Dad thinks."

* * *

Luckily for Maya, pleading and sad eyes worked better on Dad then they did on Mum.

"I suppose she could sleep up here," he said as he looked around the room. "It's got floors, proper walls, and we could put a couple of portable radiators up here," he said. He ran his hands over the exposed beams. He tried to straighten up and bumped his head off the low ceiling. "It's going to be hard getting all your stuff up here, squid. We might not fit your wardrobe up here. You OK with that? The room downstairs would be much easier."

"I really, really, *reeeeeeally* like this room. Can I have it?" said Maya.

"How are we going to get Maya's furniture up here?" asked Mum.

"It all comes apart, so we'll just carry it up bit by bit," said Dad. "Are you sure you are going to be OK, Maya?"

Maya nodded at him eagerly.

Mum and Dad looked at each other and shrugged. "Fine, we know when we are losing. But if it gets too cold, you move to the room downstairs, no arguments – agreed?" said Mum.

Maya nodded again, a huge smile breaking out across her face.

So, instead of helping Dad and Liam unload the removal van when it turned up an hour later, Mum and Maya dragged the hoover and a mop up the steep flight of stairs and did their best to clean the room. They mopped and dusted and hoovered, and Maya could hear Liam moaning that she always had to get all the attention. The room had been pretty dirty, and bits of rubbish had collected in the corners, including something that had looked oddly like a nest. But it was like no bird's nest Maya or her mother had ever seen. It had been a swirl of faded rags and downy feathers, laced with shiny pieces of paper and odd coloured stones. Maya had shuddered as her mother had swept it up, and wondered what strange kind of bird would want such a bizarre nest. Later that night, snuggling into her bed in her new room with her boxes of toys and clothes stacked up around her and the ceiling arching just over her head, she felt safe and snug. The floor was still dusty enough for her to write her name on the bare wooden boards, but she didn't care.

Mum leant down and kissed her goodnight. "Are you sure you're going to be OK up here all by yourself?" she asked.

Maya nodded, her eyelids feeling heavy with sleep.

"Well, just call me if you get scared, OK?" said Mum.

Maya smiled, her eyes closing as Mum tiptoed away and climbed down the stairs. She snuggled deep under her duvet so only her eyes were showing, and yawned as she gazed at the silvery moonlight pouring through the little window in the roof.

Just as she was drifting off to sleep, she heard a little thump on the floor next to her bed. Her eyes flew open and her body tensed. She had issues with her hearing: she got her sounds mixed up a lot. Maybe she didn't hear a thump? She swallowed. She had cleaned every inch of the attic with Mum, so it couldn't be a great big rat…

A pattering sound made her gasp and sit up in bed just in time to see teeny tiny little puffs of dust hammer the air as *something* ran from under her bed straight across the attic to the fireplace, where it disappeared.

Maya could hear nothing but her own ragged breathing in the still night air. Her heart pounded against her chest as she glared at the fireplace, daring whatever it was to come out and show itself. But nothing appeared. She had a plastic sword among her toys. She *could* get it out of its box and poke it up the chimney. But she decided that whatever was in the chimney was best left alone. She pulled the duvet over her head, in case the rat tried to run across her face in the middle of the night, and screwed her eyes tight shut. If she ignored it, it would go away.

CHAPTER TWO

The brownie sat in a niche in the chimney for what felt like half the night. His bottom was going numb from sitting so still. He was also finding it very hard not to sneeze, with all the dust and the old soot tickling his nose. Eventually the room went still and peaceful. He slowly climbed down the chimney, using his slender fingers and toes to grip the crumbly brickwork. He dropped to the ground and listened carefully, his long, tufted ears swivelling like a cat's. All he could hear was deep, rhythmic breathing.

He tiptoed over to the bed and looked at the little hand that dangled down the side. It was small and round with baby fat. He looked up and saw a little girl who had rolled right to the edge of her mattress, her face smooshed against her pillow. Her chubby cheeks were pink with sleep, and her hair was a tumbled mess of loose brown curls.

She looked very sweet, but all the same, the brownie was annoyed with her. He had lived in the attic ever since the house was built. No one had bothered with it but him, and he had the biggest space of any brownie he knew. Now *she* had to move in. Where was he supposed to live now?

He huffed with annoyance as he made his way across the room and climbed down the stairs. His big bare feet flexed on the rough wood of the landing. The carpet that had been there for years had gone, and he moved gingerly, trying not to catch his skin on splinters. Carpet nails stuck up at odd intervals, and he sliced the skin open on one side of his foot on a sneaky one that had its head half-buried in the stair, one edge popping out at an angle to catch the unwary. The little brownie gave a squeak of pain and surprise and hopped about, clutching his hurt foot between his hands. He licked the tips of his fingers with a long, pointed tongue and wiped away the beads of blood. He hobbled down the last few stairs and peered around the kitchen door, sniffing the air for any scent of a cat or a dog.

Nothing. He skipped into the kitchen and checked the hearth. No gifts for him yet, but then it was only their first night here, and he hadn't done any work yet.

Humming quietly to himself, he got to work, sweeping the dusty floors, tidying all their possessions as best he could and washing the dishes in the sink. This was his favourite job, splashing around in the warm water, scrubbing away at the pots and pans that loomed above him until he could see his reflection in their sides. He pulled the plug and felt the exciting pull of water on his toes before stacking everything as neatly as he could in the drained sink. He ran his fingertips over glasses and cups and nodded with satisfaction when they squeaked.

As the sky began to lighten and birds began to shake out their feathers and sing, he took himself back upstairs to the attic, yawning and rubbing his eyes – although he wasn't looking forward to sleeping sitting up in that niche in the chimney. He scowled. The little girl was going to have to move out.

CHAPTER THREE

Maya came down to breakfast the next morning to a room bathed in sunshine. Their new kitchen was big enough to eat in, and the windows over the sink looked out over fields, instead of the neighbours' garden wall as it had in the old flat. Their old kitchen was so shady that on a gloomy day they had to put the lights on. But here the sunlight was so strong it hurt Maya's sleep-filled eyes and made her squint.

"Just in time, sleepyhead," said Mum, who was flitting around the kitchen in a flowery apron that Maya hadn't seen before. "I've made scrambled egg on toast – your favourite."

"Except the toast is brown bread," said Dad from behind his newspaper. "*Not* your favourite."

Mum shot him a look, but unless it could cut through paper, it bounced harmlessly off *The Wiltshire Chronicle*.

"Things are going to be different now that we are here," said Mum as she put a plate of eggs in front of

Maya and then sat down opposite her at the scrubbed-pine table. Dad coughed and the paper rattled, but Mum ignored him.

"We're living in the country now, so that means we can have the country life we always dreamt of," said Mum, smiling brightly at Maya and Liam as she took a bite of her toast. Maya said nothing, just looked at the creamy golden eggs melting the butter on top of the stiff, scratchy brown-bread toast. But Liam, as usual, was happy to argue.

"That's your dream, not ours," said Liam. "I was quite happy living in the city with all my mates." He started to put his earphones in. "You only wanted us to move because of misery guts here, and let's face it, she's going to be a weirdo wherever she goes."

Maya flushed and put a forkful of egg into her mouth, while Mum frowned at Liam. "Take your earphones *out* at the table," she snapped. "You shouldn't have them in when people are talking to you anyway – it's rude. You know living in the city was bad for Maya, but frankly, I think it was bad for all of us. We're going to try a different, healthier way of life out here."

Liam sneered. "I'm not eating rabbit food because she doesn't like loud noises."

Dad slapped his newspaper down on the table, making Maya jump. "If being separated from your precious mates changes your attitude, that alone will have made the move worth all the hassle," he said, glowering at Liam, who flushed and slid down in his seat slightly. "You treat your little sister like rubbish and, despite what you might think, she understands what you say perfectly. We're *here* because it's going to be good for all of us. More space, cheaper rent, and if your mother wants to try a few recipes, then you will get to eat the new dishes and be glad *someone* wants to cook for you!"

Inside, Maya let out a little cheer, while to everyone else she looked as if she was just solemnly chewing her brown-bread toast. Dad glared at Liam until Liam looked away, and then he picked up his paper again.

"Anyway, it's not just a few recipes I want to try: I think we should really look at the way we eat," said Mum. Liam groaned, Dad sighed and Maya could feel her heart sinking (though not as quickly as the toast, which seemed to be lodging in her throat). Mum ignored them all. "We got too many takeaways in London. All that money we wasted every month!"

Maya thought longingly of KFC, the crispy, salty taste of the coating around sweet and succulent chicken drumsticks. Lamb saag from her favourite Indian take-away with free poppadoms and mint dip. Deep-pan pizza loaded up with sweetcorn, pineapple and ham... Her mouth flooded with saliva and she swallowed, hoping it would soften up the toast. There was no chance of getting a takeaway here: it was at least a twenty-five-minute drive to get to anything that looked like civilization. They didn't even have a street light out here. Maya had never lived anywhere so dark.

"And I really think we need to look at what we cook at home as well," said Mum. "It could be a lot healthier. For a start, we should cut back on the amount of pasta we eat." They all gasped and looked up at her. Mum just gazed back with an innocent expression as she buttered another slice of toast. "Don't worry, we will all survive! I think it should be more of a treat. I mean, lasagne *every* Sunday is a bit much." Dad put down his paper and stared at her, while Maya started to drool again thinking of those melting layers of cheese laid over soft sheets of pasta, gummed up with creamy béchamel sauce and yummy bolognese. She especially loved to mash her lasagne up and mix it with chips. She stabbed at her toast. She had a horrible feeling chips were going to be off the menu as well. Life was going to be very, very hard without chips.

"Now that I'm only working three days a week, I'm going to have a lot more time to do things around the house, and every meal from now on is going to be cooked from scratch. No more ready meals and no more supermarket sauces poured over yet more pasta."

"Is that why you moved us light years from a supermarket?" said Dad in a feeble attempt to make a joke, but Maya could tell he was close to tears at having his creamy carbonara sauce, his favourite Friday-night treat, taken away from him.

"And no more sweets, chocolate and fizzy drinks are going to be kept in the house," said Mum, ignoring the groans from all of them. "It is shocking how much sugar is in those things; it's so bad for us all. I'm going to bake instead!"

"Can you bake Freddo Frogs?" asked Liam, his voice dripping with sarcasm. Maya and Dad couldn't help it: they both spluttered out a laugh before Mum's hurt expression made them choke it back.

"No one is asking you lot to do any of the cooking," said Mum in a small, sharp, slightly angry voice that made Maya want to pull her head into her shoulders like a tortoise. "So, unless anyone wants to volunteer to do all the shopping and cooking?…" Silence reigned. "I thought not. And Liam, stop blaming your sister for everything you do not like in your life."

Dad patted his stomach. "I think we could all do with fewer takeaways, and it's going to be nice to have more time to cook special meals. I used to love cooking."

Mum took a sip of her tea and gazed at them, a small smile hovering around her lips. "Anyway, this move has already made a change in somebody."

They all looked back at her, puzzled, while Mum looked at each of them in turn questioningly.

"Well, come on, own up!" she said. "It's hardly like I'm going to be angry, is it?"

"Own up to what?" asked Liam, a frown furrowing his face.

"In what is a first in this family, someone, other than me, cleaned up the kitchen last night," said Mum. "It was a really lovely surprise when I came downstairs this morning! So come on, who did it? They're going to get a big fat kiss!"

"Don't look at me," mumbled Liam. Dad just shrugged when Mum looked at him. Maya felt her cheeks grow warm when Mum smiled at her. "It must have been you then, squid. What a thoughtful girl you are!"

"It wasn't me," said Maya.

Mum laughed. "Of course it was you, squid! Who else could it be?"

She knew she shouldn't have said it, even as the words came blurting out, but the answer just seemed so obvious. "It was probably the thing in my room."

"What thing?" said Dad, tipping the paper so he could look at her over the top of it.

"Something was running around my room last night, and it had two legs, so it wasn't a mouse. It ran into my fireplace."

Liam snorted with laughter, while Dad raised an eyebrow. Mum began to smile again while understanding dawned on her face.

"Oh, I see, you have an invisible friend," she said. "How wonderful!"

Liam sneered again. "What's so fantastic about her making up a friend because she hasn't got any real ones? It just proves she's a weirdo."

"Actually, Liam, having an invisible friend is very important to the development of a child. It stimulates their imagination and helps them to explore the world in ways they understand," said Mum. "You had one when you were a little bit younger than Maya." She looked at Dad with an expression of mock seriousness on her face. "What was he called again?"

"Mr Snuggles," said Dad, winking at Maya. She began to giggle. Liam blushed, his face furious.

"What is your friend called, Maya?" asked Mum. Maya shrugged.

"Whoever they are, if they encourage you to clean the house, they're a fantastic friend to have around as far as I am concerned," said Mum. "The next time you and your friend want to play, the windows need cleaning."

Maya looked at the cold toast. "Could I have porridge tomorrow?"

"Only if I'm making it for everyone else, squid," said Mum, taking another sip of her tea. "I'm not making separate meals for everyone."

Maya escaped back up the stairs to her room as soon as her plate was cleared. She looked at her blue school rucksack, tossed into the corner next to a pile of boxes. Her fingers twitched, but she thought, *No. I'm not going to eat anything. I'm going to make it last.*

She cocked her head and listened to the silence that seemed to press in around the little house from all sides. Just birds and trees bending and swaying in a summer breeze. She couldn't even hear traffic, the main road was so far away.

She really hoped Mum hadn't made them move because she thought noise upset her. She had funny ears; the doctor told Mum they were all glued up and she couldn't hear sounds that were very high and very low. But she *could* hear, and noise didn't upset her. She just got upset when noise got jumbled up. Sometimes she didn't hear car engines very well because they made deep, rumbling sounds, but that upset Mum, not her. The time she had really got upset was when she had gone to the playground with Mum and all the other children had started talking to her at once: all their voices got mixed up together so that all she could hear was a jangling, roaring noise. She had started crying, so in a way Liam was right: it *was* her fault they had moved, because she was sure that was when Mum had decided they were going to leave the city.

But the silence was worse. It was a physical thing that pressed down on Maya and filled her mouth, her ears, her nose. It was *heavy*, especially in the velvety darkness, when the only sounds were odd animal cries that she didn't recognize. The city, at night, had hummed and babbled with noise that was a constant, flowing stream, and it had rocked her to sleep in her little boxroom, with all her things wrapped around her. She wiggled her fingers, distracted, and glanced again at her school bag.

One little bite, she thought. *I have to make it last.*

Shoulders hunched with guilt, she scurried over to her bag, with a backward glance over her shoulder to make sure no one was climbing the stairs to her room. She unzipped it and felt for a thin plastic bag at the bottom and pulled it out. She opened it up and stared at the purple-and-silver wrappers of the chocolate bars.

Now that chocolate was beginning to look like an endangered species in her life, she thought she finally knew how Charlie had felt in *Charlie and the Chocolate Factory*. Those six chocolate bars were looking as precious as gold to her now that she didn't know when she could get any more. Auntie Cass had shoved them into her bag when she had come round to the flat to say goodbye. "I'm going to miss you lot like mad," she had said, her eyes wet with unshed tears. "Can't pop around whenever I feel like to spoil you rotten, so this lot is going to have to keep you going until I can make my way out to the sticks to see you all." Maya had nodded, the love she felt for Aunt Cass as sweet and sugary as a Dairy Milk.

Maya sighed and carefully unwrapped the top of the chocolate bar, gently peeled back the wrapping and broke off one square. She popped it into her mouth and just let it sit on her tongue. The thick slab of chocolate melted slowly, spreading out to gum up against her teeth, sticking her tongue to the roof of her mouth. She sat there for long moments, her eyes half-closed, and savoured the rich taste before swallowing the sweet sludge. She sighed and looked at the bar in her hand.

I need to save this, she thought. *I'll be good and just eat one square of chocolate a day. It will last for aaaages that way.* She bit her lip and then broke off square after square, popping them into her mouth one by one and chewing on them, licking the tip of her finger and chasing the last few crumbs left clinging to the wrapping.

She looked around the room guiltily. *Tomorrow. I'll start making them last tomorrow.* She crumpled the wrapper into a tiny ball and shoved it into the pocket of her jeans.

CHAPTER FOUR

The brownie woke up in the blackest part of the night, cramped, stiff and in a very bad mood. He had had a nice bed before the girl and her mother had swept it up. Old rags had made it soft, and he had lined it with bird feathers to make it warm and downy. He had been surrounded by all his precious things, and at night he had dragged the nest into the moonbeams that filtered through the small window, lain in his bed and marvelled at the colours of his treasures. *All gone*, he thought, with a hard lump in his throat, *destroyed in seconds by that loud woman and that little sneak of a girl.*

The chimney was cold comfort, a hard and dirty bed. His nose itched as tiny little particles of soot ticked the sensitive skin inside his nostrils. It coated his body as well, and he would need a wash in the sink before he could start his chores tonight. He had waited for hours for the little girl to go to sleep. At one point, just as he had been about to climb down into the dusty fireplace, she had woken up, white-faced and panicking as a fox barked somewhere in the fields outside her bedroom. He had dangled upside down, his long toes clinging on to the loose brick of the chimney, and had watched her clutching at her duvet, panting with fear as the fox called. He was ready to pull his head up in the dark if she looked his way, but she had only stared, bewildered, at the bare window. He had frowned, wondering at her terror, and then it dawned on him – she was frightened of the fox! He stuck his tongue out at her as she settled down again into her warm, soft bed. Silly goose! Who was frightened of foxes calling?

He had dozed off again waiting for her to drift back into a deep and dreamless sleep. When he awoke with a start, he realized that the velvety black his eyes had snapped open into was the dark that came before the dawn. He didn't have long if he wanted to clean up before the house woke up.

Grumbling, he slipped out of the chimney and hopped from foot to foot on the chilly stone hearth. He looked longingly at the blue bag that was propped against the little girl's bed, and his mouth watered as he remembered that sweet, rich smell of the food she kept in there. He licked his lips at the thought of tasting just a morsel. But brownies didn't steal. They were rewarded for their hard work, normally with a bowl of porridge, sweetened with a drop of honey. But if the new household wanted to give him some of the lovely food he could smell from here, he wouldn't be complaining.

That thought cheered him up no end, and he positively skipped down the attic stairs. He tutted at the sight of all the work to be done. Boxes packed with possessions were still piled everywhere, the dusting hadn't been done and the floors were crunchy underfoot. He sighed. The brownie couldn't stand a mess. No brownie could; it was their nature. He wouldn't get the whole house done tonight, but he worked hard on the sitting room, cleaning and tidying at a dizzying speed so that when he finally stepped back with a satisfied sigh the whole room looked as if it had been given a good bath. He even took time to clean the lead-paned window, carefully wiping down each square of glass. But when he came to the last one, he hesitated.

The old lady who had lived here before had been kind to him. She had left a bowl of porridge for him every night in the kitchen. And she had also talked to him as he flitted through the shadows of the house, dogging her footsteps. She had never tried to see him – that would have been very rude: the brownie did not want to be seen. But she knew he was there, and she told him all about the world outside and even sang to him, in her thin, cracked voice, as she sat in her chair by the sitting room. The brownie had watched as she gazed into the fire, his eyes glowing like a cat's in the firelight.

He had been her house brownie for many years, and they knew each other's ways. Although brownies were solitary creatures, he was surprised to find his stomach lurched, just a little, when he thought of the old lady. These people were new. Perhaps they hadn't had a brownie living with them before? He supposed he should try and be nice, let them know what they were supposed to do. So although he had dusted and polished the glass of the window until it squeaked when he rubbed it with a fingertip, he had left one pane dusty and carefully traced a word in the dirt.

Porridge.

CHAPTER FIVE

Maya did not sleep well that night. She had tossed and turned in her bed until the duvet had wrapped itself around her, hot and clammy as dough. She couldn't get used to the silence of the countryside or the heart-stopping way that silence would be broken by the odd shrieks from animals and birds. It was like nothing she had ever heard before, and as she hovered in a light sleep, these dreams pierced her mind and her imagination made them into the cries of hairy, bloodthirsty monsters that prowled the fields that surrounded their small cottage.

When she finally woke up, her eyes itching from lack of sleep and her head heavy and aching, she noticed that the attic room was getting warm and that the sun was blazing through the window. She had slept most of the morning away. Grumpy, she kicked the sweat-soaked duvet off her legs and staggered towards the stairs, following the sound of her mother's voice to the kitchen.

Liam was in the sitting room, his trainer-clad feet on the sofa, which would make Mum go mad if she saw. His earphones were clamped into his ears as usual, the tinny sound of music drifting over to Maya in the doorway. She hated Liam's taste in music and didn't see how his iPod could be called a personal device if she could hear everything all the time. She shuffled past into the kitchen, where her mum was unpacking shopping from bags she didn't recognize. No Sainsbury's, no Tesco, no Morrisons. This couldn't be good.

Sure enough, all of the things that Mum was busy storing in cupboards in the kitchen looked about as yummy as cardboard. Maya watched glumly as bags of lentils went on shelves, brown bread in the bread bin, hummus into the fridge. There was flour and caster sugar, but no cookies. There was couscous and rice, but no potatoes. No white bread, no sticky sweet jam, no biscuits at all, but lots of fruit. Maya stole a quick glance at Dad, who looked as gloomy as she felt. Mum didn't seem to notice.

"…The natural food shop is just amazing, the prices are not too bad and it's just like shopping in the supermarket, as they had everything we wanted…"

You wanted, Maya corrected her mother silently.

"…Shopping there is a bit of an education too: they have leaflets all around the store telling you about things like the harm food additives can do – and did you know the damage palm-oil companies are causing in places like Indonesia?" Mum stopped talking for a second and looked at Dad, who just shook his head.

"I got chatting with the store manager, and he was telling me how bad dairy is for us," Mum went on. "He was saying that we were not supposed to drink milk after weaning, and that was why there were so many dairy allergies. They sell almond milk at the store – do you think we should start using that instead of semi-skimmed?"

Dad and Maya looked at each other in total panic. What was Mum going to get rid of now?!

"Why don't we try out new things one at a time?" said Dad. "I don't think I am ready to give up milk just yet."

Mum frowned. "It's just a suggestion," she said.

"I know," said Dad. "But perhaps it would be easier if we didn't make too many changes at the same time."

Maya nodded, as it dawned on her that, without milk, there would be no hot chocolate. She felt shaky with relief as she remembered she still had hot chocolate in her life. Dad had actually gone white for a few minutes. Maya bit back a giggle as she realized he had gone the same colour as milk.

"Anyway, this move has already brought about a big change in someone," said Mum. She smiled at them both. "Come on, who did it?"

Maya and Dad looked at each other, puzzled.

"Oh, come on, you can admit to it, I am hardly going to be angry, am I?" said Mum, laughing.

"If it makes you happy, I'll admit to it," said Dad. "But honestly, I don't know what you are talking about."

"Oh, come on! Neither of you remembers getting up and cleaning the kitchen last night as a surprise?" said Mum. "I know Liam didn't do it: it has to be one of you."

"Not me," said Dad.

"I didn't do it," said Maya.

"No, we know," said Dad. "It was your invisible friend, right?" He winked at her. Normally Maya liked it when Dad winked at her, but today it just really annoyed her.

"It's not funny!" she said. "*You* try sleeping with something creepy in your room!"

"Maya, I was only joking…" said Dad, as Liam walked into the kitchen.

"What's wrong with her now?" he asked.

"It seems she doesn't get on with her invisible friend," said Mum.

Liam shook his head. "Only *you* can fall out with your invisible friend," he snorted.

Maya looked at them all in frustration, burst into tears and ran from the room.

"What on earth has got into her?" she heard Mum ask.

Maya ran all the way back to her bedroom, slamming her bedroom door hard. She sat on her bed, her arms wrapped around her knees, and sobbed. She hated this new house, hated the way Mum wanted to change everything now that they had moved, and she bet she was going to hate her new school in September. She couldn't wait to grow up and move back to London! They all wanted her to talk and make friends, but what was the point if no one ever listened to her? Parents were supposed to make everything better, but Mum and Dad were making everything worse, and she was so angry they wouldn't believe her about the thing in her room. It scared her, and she hardly slept at night.

Her stomach growled so loudly while she cried that it was like there were two people in the room. So, although she was pretty fed up with everyone in her family right now, she was still grateful to hear footsteps on the attic stairway and the smell of toast. She was less happy to see that the person bringing her breakfast was Liam and the toast was, once again, brown bread.

"Don't cry, squid," he said as he handed her the plate and the glass of orange juice. "I don't like it here much either, but there's not a lot we can do about it. If we're lucky, Mum will get sick of the country and be desperate to move back to London by Christmas."

Maya sniffed and said nothing, chewing hard on the rough, grainy bread.

"It's not my fault we moved, you know," she said after a minute.

Liam huffed. "Doesn't seem like that. Did London really mess up your hearing that much?"

She looked at her food. "It was bad when there was too much noise. Then everything sort of mashed together until I couldn't hear anything clearly, even if someone was standing right in front of me talking. School is horrible, because everyone just yells and screams all the time and I can't hear anything. That's why I kept getting in trouble with the teacher – she said I was ignoring her, but I wasn't."

"What's it like here then – any better with all this peace and quiet?"

Maya thought about it for a moment. "I can hear stuff better, but with no background noise, like there always was in London, it all sounds – *heavier*, somehow."

Liam sighed, lay back on the bed and laced his fingers behind his head. "I think it was the same for Mum and Dad. They were always talking about how cramped they felt in London, how there was no space, how all the noise got on their nerves. Do you remember the way people would be stuck in traffic outside the flat and their music would be going full blast all day long during the summer? Used to drive Dad nuts when he was trying to get some work done."

Maya winced. She remembered it too well – it was one of the things she hated about summer.

"It probably will be better here, you know," said Maya. "I think it's nice that Mum can afford to go part time and Dad doesn't have to work such long hours. We'll see a lot more of them."

"S'pose," said Liam. He looked around the room. "It's nice up here," he said. "Lots of space." He thought for a second. "My mates could come and visit – there would be plenty of room for them to kip on the floor up here."

Maya scowled. "They can sleep in the spare room."

"No way," Liam said, laughing. "What bloke is going to want to sleep in a pink room?"

"You're not blokes," Maya pointed out. "You're boys."

"Still, it can't be very nice for you up here, all by yourself," said Liam with a sly look on his face. "All these weird noises this house makes at night must scare you stiff. You're miles away from Mum and Dad if, you know, anything happened."

Maya stopped chewing for a second and looked at him, her stomach tingling with fear. "Like what?"

Liam shrugged. "Who knows what's creeping around an old house like this?" said Liam. "Someone could have *died* in here and their ghost could be hanging about. Who knows what that thing is that's hanging about your room?"

Maya swallowed the last of her orange juice and handed the empty glass and her crumb-strewn plate back to her brother, trying not to let him see her hands shaking.

"I'm not moving out of my room," she said, in a quiet but determined voice.

Liam winked at her, just like Dad, but only much, much more annoying. "We'll see."

She glared at him as he walked across the room, turned and began to climb backwards down the steep stairs. He gave her a cheery little wave before disappearing through the floor, and she stuck her tongue out at the empty air where his face had just been.

A small, shuffling, rustling noise caught her ear, and she whipped her head round in time to see her school rucksack moving gently, as if something small was tugging at the zip. She lunged across the room and snatched it up into her arms, hearing a frightened little squeak and that familiar patter of tiny feet as whatever it was retreated under her bed. Not a rat then. Rats couldn't open zips.

She zipped the bag closed again and hugged it to herself.

"NOBODY is making me leave," she said.

There was only silence in her room, but it sounded like the silence was listening.

CHAPTER SIX

It had been cool and shady under the girl's bed, even if the brownie had to sleep on the rock-hard floorboards. *Still*, he thought, *it was no harder than the bricks in the chimney.* He waited until the house was dark and quiet and scooted out from under the bed, easing his slight body onto the top step by balancing on his stomach and then dropping onto the steep step below.

As he started to head for the stairs that would lead him to the kitchen, his empty stomach growled so loudly that he froze on the spot, eyes wide with fear, bat-like ears swivelling to catch every sound in the sleeping house. His stomach growled again, and he clasped it with both hands, hoping to muffle the noise. Surely someone must have heard that?

But only the sounds of deep, rhythmic breathing came from the bedrooms. The household was still sleeping; his presence remained unnoticed. He breathed a soft sigh of relief and made his way downstairs.

He padded into the living room on his bare feet and wrinkled his nose at the mess. Discarded clothes, toys, books and magazines lay scattered around. They hadn't even put the cushions straight on the sofa! Not a single box seemed to have been unpacked as far as he could see. He sighed. It was going to be a long night. But he needed to eat first.

Making his way to the kitchen, the brownie sniffed eagerly for the scent of porridge, either warming on the stove or cooling in a bowl on the hearth. But all he could smell was dirty dishes, and he stopped in the middle of the kitchen and looked around him in dismay. Two nights of work and nothing left out for him, not even a raisin!

He stuffed a fist into his mouth and gnawed on it in hunger and frustration. He was so very hungry! Then he narrowed his eyes. This wasn't fair. He had done his work, had even left them a hint, and yet they didn't do what they were supposed to. Brownies didn't steal, but they were allowed to cause mischief if they were not treated well by their household.

The brownie chuckled and used his little hands and feet to cling to the kitchen cupboards. Up, up he climbed, to the cupboards that smelt so deliciously of food. Nose snuffling, he opened a door and then scooped the contents onto the floor. A bag of flour burst and formed a cloud for a split second; lentils spilt across the flagstones with the rustling hiss of snakeskin; herbs and spices followed quickly, tipped out from little glass jars to add more puffing little clouds in orange and brown and green clouds. The smell was heavenly, and the little brownie's stomach growled even louder.

He climbed down and forced the fridge door open. Shivering with cold, he climbed up to the top half of the door and gleefully flung eggs into the mess in the middle of the floor. The fragile shells cracked open with a satisfying splat, and the yellow yolks puddled in the flour. The brownie jumped down and shuffled and danced through the mess, wagging his little hips as he ground the eggs beneath his feet, his long fingers tapping a beat in the air as he hummed a tune. When he had emptied out nearly all the cupboards and spread the mess across the entire kitchen floor, he carefully bit open a box of porridge oats and spread them across the top of the kitchen table. With his fingertip he wrote two words: NO PORRIDGE.

He smiled grimly and nodded. *Now they'll know and they will be sorry!* he thought. He looked at the mess and sighed. It didn't help his poor stomach, though. He jumped down from the table and wiped his feet on a clean bit of flagstone so he would not leave a trail. Head drooping and stomach growling ferociously, he climbed the stairs to the attic, up to his little ledge. As he tried to get comfortable on the hard, cold brick, a little tear cut through his flour-dusted face. He thought of the old lady again, the warm fire and her cracked voice. He thought longingly of the sweet porridge she always used to make, with a bit of cream on good days and a sprinkle of raisins. As his stomach growled louder and louder, he laid his cheek against the sooty brick and cried.

CHAPTER SEVEN

"UP!"

Maya was startled awake the next morning by her mother yanking back the duvet. She stood over the bed with a very angry expression on her face. Maya scrambled out and onto the floorboards, her face flushing. She couldn't think what she had done wrong, but she felt guilty anyway.

Her mother pointed at the gap in the floor. "Downstairs to the kitchen, NOW!"

Gulping nervously, Maya scuttled ahead, her stomach flip-flopping as her mind raced to think of what she could have done. Could it be the chocolate hidden in her rucksack? But then, why was Mum making her go to the kitchen? She trotted on in front of her mother, who climbed down the stairs with hard, angry steps and banged the landing door shut behind her. But as soon as she saw the mess the kitchen was in, her mouth dropped open and she stared, speechless.

It was like a bomb had gone off. Cupboard doors hung open and, as far as Maya could tell, all the shopping her mother had done was now lying on the floor in a greyish-brown mess – a greyish-brown mess that smelt, oddly enough, like cake. Her father was looking at her with a very disappointed expression, while Liam was looking at her with a *really* odd expression – admiration.

Maya turned to face her mother as she marched into the room behind her. "I didn't do it!"

"Well, I didn't do it and your father didn't, so that just leaves you and Liam," said Mum. She crossed her arms over her chest. "You've got five seconds to tell me which one of you did this."

"It wasn't me!" Maya protested again. Dad sighed.

"Look, it wasn't me – I've got better things to be doing with my time – so just admit to it," said Liam.

"I'll be much angrier if you lie to me," said Mum. "You know I hate being lied to. And before you blame your brother, perhaps you can explain *that*." Mum pointed at the kitchen table, and Maya looked down and read the words drawn into the spilt porridge oats with a sinking heart.

"Liam doesn't like porridge – maybe he wrote it," said Maya.

Liam rolled his eyes, while Dad sighed and Mum's lips pressed into a thin white line.

"You two had better tell me which one of you is responsible for this or you'll be spending the day in your rooms!" said Mum.

"It wasn't me!" said Liam and Maya at the same time.

"It had to be *someone*," said Dad.

Maya looked at them all and swallowed nervously. "It was probably that thing that lives in my room," she said in a tiny voice. Mum and Dad looked annoyed, but Liam's face brightened.

"So it *was* you!" said Mum. "Why can't you just say that?"

"But—" Maya began, but Mum interrupted her.

"It's nice that you're using your imagination to make a friend, but don't think for one moment you can behave badly and blame it on them," said Mum.

"But—" said Maya.

"You are in big trouble over this, young lady. You have spoilt a lot of food, and it's going to cost a lot of money to replace it all. You can spend the rest of the day in your room while your father and I think about a suitable punishment."

Liam looked at the mess again and gave Maya a thumbs-up. "Respect, squid," he said. "I didn't know you had it in you."

"Liam, you are not helping," said Dad.

"IT'S NOT FAIR!" shouted Maya, and ran back to her room sobbing, for the second day in a row.

Up in her room she cried for what seemed like hours, until her eyes were swollen to the size of tennis balls and were hot and gritty. The delicious smell of sweet porridge cooked with milk, sugar crystals melting in its heat, wafted its way up the stairs. Liam rose up through the floor, a steaming bowl held high in his hand.

"No need to look surprised – you don't think Mum was going to let you starve, did you?"

He sat down beside her and handed her the bowl. Maya began to spoon it into her mouth.

"Is Mum really angry?" she asked, her mouth full.

"Pretty much," said Liam. "That was some stunt you pulled."

Maya's cheeks were already hot and red from the crying, but she flushed a darker crimson.

"I *told* you…" she said.

"Yeah, yeah, I know, your invisible friend did it," said Liam. He stood up and stretched. "I don't care how you are doing it, but keep up the good work. The more you wind Mum up, the more likely it is she'll kick you out and give me this room."

Liam gave that annoying wink again and walked out of the room.

Maya sighed and put her spoon down. She thought about the words written in the porridge oats (she really hoped Mum had used a fresh box to make breakfast with, not the ones that had been lying on the table) and why the thing in her room would have made all that mess. She thought about all the cleaning that had been done in the two nights before the kitchen had become a crime scene. She thought about the little nest she and Mum had swept up.

She looked at the chimney. *So no food, for three days?* she thought.

She put the bowl down on the floor and tore open one of the cardboard boxes that held her toys. She rummaged around until she found a little plastic bowl from her tea set and a tiny spoon. She carefully poured some of the warm porridge into the little bowl and carried it over to the fireplace. She put the bowl down on the cast-iron hearth and watched as sugar-scented steam drifted up into the dark chimney.

"I'm sorry," she whispered. "I didn't know you were hungry – I would have brought you something. You can share my breakfast with me if you like. But please don't make any more mess, because my mummy will be angry and she might make me move out and give this room to my brother. He won't believe in you, and he smells like sweaty trainers."

There was no sound from the chimney. Maya thought the little creature might want to eat alone. He certainly didn't seem to like being seen. So she picked up her own bowl, closed her bedroom door behind her and ate her porridge sitting on the stairs.

CHAPTER EIGHT

The bricks did not get any softer, but the little brownie certainly found it easier to sleep with a full stomach. He woke up and patted his full tummy happily, his little pot belly still stretched tight with lovely sweet porridge.

He climbed down from his perch and tiptoed across the room to look at the girl. She was fast asleep, her arms and legs flung wide, the duvet kicked off her sleeping form. Her pyjama legs and sleeves had scrunched up, and it made her look as if she was bursting out of her clothes. Her brown curls tumbled all about her and snaked over the edge of her pillow. Her cheeks were rosy with sleep. He leant in and took a deep breath. She smelt of sugar and honey and milk. He wrinkled his nose. He didn't want a boy who smelt of trainers to move in instead. And if this boy didn't believe in him, there would be no porridge left on the hearth.

His mind made up, the little brownie made his way down the stairs from the attic. But instead of carrying

46

on downstairs, he padded over to the boy's bedroom door. It hadn't been closed properly, and it swung open slightly at the gentlest push from his hand. His long fingers gripped the edge, and he peered around, blinking his huge eyes as they adjusted to the dark of the room. The boy was fast asleep, and he scooted quickly inside and closed the door behind him.

He clapped a hand over his nose and tried not to breathe in. The little girl wasn't wrong about the smell! There was on overpowering odour of sweaty trainers, dirty clothes and a sickly-sweet smell that the brownie couldn't place. He took a breath and turned a little green, but his super-sensitive nose led him over to a very messy chest of drawers that looked like it was spitting out clothes. The brownie climbed the open drawers like a ladder and flipped the lid off a can and took a sniff at the nozzle. He gagged at the cloying smell, stuck his tongue out and frantically pawed at it to get the smell off his taste buds.

He put his head to one side and read the words on the side of the can – Lynx Attract. He put the lid back on to stop the smell and scratched at his head, puzzled. He had read the books the old lady had kept in the house, especially the wildlife ones. He had read about lynxes, wildcats that lived in Scotland. They looked very pretty, but why a human boy would want to smell like one he didn't understand. He squinted at the can – how did they get the smell of the lynx in there in the first place?

He shrugged and began to climb back down the drawers, pulling what he hoped were clean clothes with him as he went. All night he flitted in and out of the room, in and out of the house, taking clothes, those sweaty trainers, those stupid noisy things that he thought were permanently attached to the boy's ears and stank of earwax. As the sky began to lighten, he piled all the dirty clothes into a heap on the floor and nodded with satisfaction. Yawning and rubbing his eyes, he headed back to his niche in the chimney. As he curled up on the bare brick, his tummy fizzed with glee – it was a shame he wouldn't be awake to see the look on the boy's face. He curled up and drifted into sleep, a smile on his lips.

CHAPTER NINE

"Maya, you'd better get down here, RIGHT NOW!"

The sound of her brother's bellowing voice startled Maya awake. She sat bolt upright in bed, her hair messy and standing on end.

"Do NOT go up to her room. Dad will get her and then we'll talk about this," she heard Mum say.

Confused and still very sleepy, Maya looked up at Dad as he walked into the room. He was frowning and trying to look strict, but Maya could see that he was struggling not to laugh.

"What's up?" she asked.

Dad almost burst out laughing, but he covered his mouth with his hand and pretended he was coughing.

"Quite a bit actually," he said. "Maya, were you in Liam's room last night?"

Maya frowned. "No."

"Are you sure?"

She nodded as she heard Mum's and Liam's footsteps thunder down the bare wooden stairs and out of the front door.

"Um, can you come outside for a second?" asked Dad. "There is something I would like you to see."

Maya got out of bed and followed Dad downstairs, yawning and rubbing her eyes. She followed him out of the front door and stopped dead on the doorstep, her jaw dropping. Liam was silent but red with rage, and Mum was covering her mouth with one hand. "Do you think you could explain this?" she asked, her eyes sparkling with laughter as she waved at the tree in their front garden.

It looked as if everything Liam owned was hanging in the tree. But hanging very neatly, Maya noticed. His trainers and his football boots had been tied together with their laces and hung over a branch. His earphones were draped over another. Every pair of jeans, every T-shirt and every sweatshirt he owned had been folded and hung like a bizarre Christmas decoration. Sparrows twittered among the thick summer leaves, and Maya noticed a white streak of bird poo down the front of Liam's favourite black T-shirt. She clapped her hands over her mouth in horror when she saw it, and then the laughter came bubbling up from her tummy. She spluttered as she tried to hold it in, and then silvery peals of laughter broke out of her.

Mum and Dad looked at each other and burst into laughter themselves, doubling over and holding their stomachs. Dad was actually crying, he was laughing so hard.

"IT'S NOT FUNNY!" shouted Liam.

"It is!" wheezed Mum, breathless from laughing. "It really is."

"How did you do it, squid?" asked Dad.

"Yeah," said Liam, his voice low and threatening. "How *did* you do it?"

"I didn't," said Maya. She felt a little annoyed at the disbelief in their faces, so she walked over to the tree and pointed out the obvious. "Look!" she said, and jumped as high as she could with her fingertips outstretched. They didn't touch the lowest branch.

They looked at her, and worry began to cloud her mother's face. "She can't reach," she said.

"She must have climbed – any idiot can climb a tree!" said Liam.

"All night?" asked Dad. "Are you seriously suggesting that your sister spent the whole night taking stuff from your room and climbing this tree in the dark to hang everything up?!"

Liam looked at Dad, and his mouth opened and closed like a goldfish's, but no noise came out.

"Maya, sweetie, do you know who did do this?" asked Mum.

Maya shrugged. "It must be the thing that's living in my room," she said.

"Oh, come on!" said Liam. "Not this invisible-friend story again."

"Why would your friend want to play a trick like this on Liam, squid?" asked Dad.

"I don't know," said Maya. "Maybe because Liam said he was going to get you guys to make me move into the spare room so he could live in the attic. I don't think he wants Liam to move into that room." Her parents glared at Liam.

"Have you been tormenting your sister?" asked Dad, in a very quiet but angry voice – the kind of voice that told you he had already lost his temper and you were in big trouble. Liam went pale and swallowed nervously.

"No," he said. "I just thought that room was a bit scary for her, all on her own."

"Oh, just thinking of your sister, were you?" asked Dad. "I tell you what – why don't you help me get all your stuff out of this tree and then you can clean your room and really get to enjoy spending some time in there?"

"Come on, Maya," said Mum, holding out her hand. "Let's get you some breakfast."

"Can I have porridge again?" asked Maya.

"Sure."

"Can I eat it in my room and share it with my friend?"

Mum's smile wavered for just a second. "Sure."

Up in her room, Maya poured a little of the porridge into a plastic bowl and put it on the hearth with a doll's spoon balanced on the rim. She got down on her hands and knees and poked her head into the chimney.

"Thank you for doing that," she whispered. "Liam was really annoyed, but Mum and Dad know he was trying to take this room now, so he will have to leave us alone. I hope you like the porridge – I asked Mum to put a bit of cream in it."

Just like the day before, she picked up her own bowl and let herself out of the attic to sit on the stairs and eat her porridge out of sight and sound of the shy little creature who lived in her room.

* * *

Maya was lying on her stomach in their new back garden, her head propped up in her hands, squinting into the hot sunshine as she watched a fluffy bumblebee nuzzle at the lavender flowers on a spreading bush, when Dad's shadow fell over her.

He sat down next to her and watched the bee for a moment.

"Nature-watching, are we?" he asked.

"Mmmmm," said Maya, as she went back to watching the little bee flit from flower to flower, humming away to itself as it worked.

"Do you like bees?"

"Yeah. They're like little teddy bears," said Maya. "I wish I could cuddle them."

Dad laughed and ruffled her hair with one hand. "I wouldn't try it."

They sat there in a comfortable silence for a while, watching as the bee got giddier and giddier on pollen, and then Dad said, "I know this move has been tough for you, squid."

Maya felt her heart sink. This was the start of a Serious Talk. Maya hated Serious Talks.

"It's hard to get used to a new place, for anyone," Dad went on. "You miss your friends, you miss your favourite places, and I bet you're not looking forward to starting a new school and being the new kid in the class, are you?"

Maya kept on staring at the bee, but she shook her head.

"The house is weird too – all those strange noises it makes at night," said Dad. Maya looked at him in surprise. She didn't realize Dad was listening to the same things as her. "We're not used to being in an old house," he continued. "They're different from new places, all the creaks and groans the wood makes as the house cools down at night, the strange noises that come from old pipes forced round bends and corners in a place that was never built for pipes..."

"There's noises outside too," whispered Maya.

"Yeah, the countryside isn't as quiet as I thought," said Dad. "And then there's the dark. Why does it have to be so *dark*?"

Maya looked up at him and smiled as he shook his head in mock confusion.

"Mum's been going a bit overboard with this health-food thing as well, hasn't she?" asked Dad.

Maya screwed up her face and squinted into the sun. She really, really wanted to say yes, but she didn't want to sound like she was talking about Mum behind her back. But oh, how she missed chips! She could feel Dad looking at her and knew he was probably smiling. He nudged her.

"You don't think so, eh?" he asked. "You're really enjoying all the brown bread and rice? Don't miss pizzas or burgers or chips or pasta?"

She kept her mouth shut tight and tried not to drool as she thought about all that food. "I think I like brown bread now," said Maya. "It's got more taste than white. Especially when I cover it in honey."

"That's good," said Dad in a cheery voice. "You won't mind when Mum starts making her own soup, then? She's talking about making fennel soup."

Maya looked up at him, her eyes wide. "What's fennel?"

"It's a sort of vegetable," said Dad. "Tastes like liquorice."

She couldn't help it. Just the thought of eating soup that tasted like liquorice made Maya shudder, stick her tongue out and make gagging noises, while Dad laughed.

"How about I talk to Mum – maybe we could have a few unhealthy meals every now and then?" asked Dad. "Perhaps she could be persuaded to have a bag of chips in the freezer? I'll have a word with Liam – nobody is going to force you out of your room. In return, perhaps you could get your little friend to behave?"

Maya frowned. "I don't know if I can."

"You said it's living in the chimney, right?" asked Dad. Maya nodded. "Well, I was thinking that couldn't be very comfortable. You wouldn't fancy sleeping on bricks all night, would you?"

Maya shrugged, but with a sinking heart she realized her father was right. She would hate to give up her lovely, soft, warm bed at night, and yet she had been letting her mysterious friend sleep in the cold, dirty chimney. She knew they had destroyed his bed, but she hadn't thought to get him a new one.

Dad smiled at her. "Do you think you could make up a comfy bed for your friend, something he would never want to get out of, like yourself and Liam?"

"I think so," said Maya, her mind running through her toys and doll things to see what would suit her little friend.

"Hopefully having a proper bed again will make your friend sleepy at night, so there will be no more tricks played on your brother."

Maya shrugged again.

"Think about it, squid," her dad said. "Everyone will settle in better if your little friend sleeps every night."

CHAPTER TEN

The brownie was dozing fitfully as the sun went down, his head bent at an awkward angle, his chin touching his chest. The sound of the little girl's voice drifting up through the dust of the chimney woke him up. He rubbed the sleep from his eyes and the drool from his chin and cocked an ear to hear better.

"Thank you again for what you did last night," she whispered in that small voice of hers. "I thought you might like this." There was a rustling noise, and something very, very sweet was placed on the hearth. The little brownie leant forward so far, his nose snuffling the air eagerly and his eyes sparkling with greed, that he almost fell off his little ledge.

"I've got another surprise for you as well, something special," said the little girl. "I think you will really like it, but I can't put it in the chimney, so I have left it under my bed. I'm going to go to sleep now, and I am going to shut my eyes really, really tight and make sure I fall asleep quickly, so you can look at it. Night-night."

The brownie was so busy sniffing at that heavenly scent that he almost forgot and said "Night-night" back. But he clapped a hand over his mouth and stopped the words escaping just in time. Brownies were meant to be a secret in their household, even if everyone knew they were there. It wouldn't do to talk to a human.

He wrapped his arms around himself and rocked backwards and forwards on his ledge. The smell of the food she had left was filling up the whole chimney, and he had to keep swallowing as saliva filled his mouth. He listened to the sounds of her bedtime routine, waited for her parents to come in to read her a story and kiss her goodnight. He waited for the night to grow darker and the house stiller, for all the noises the family made in the evening to fall away gradually, until all he could hear was the house breathing in and out to the sounds of their sleeping. Then, and only then, did he climb down the sides of the chimney, as fast as he could, to snatch up the thing that smelt so good.

It was wrapped up in purple-and-white paper, and he shredded it between his little fingers in his haste to pull it off. It was a brown square chunk of something that crumbled slightly at the edges when he touched it. Carefully, he stretched out his tongue and licked it.

He almost swooned as his taste buds jangled. If he had thought sugary porridge had been a treat, this food was *stuffed* with sugar! Just licking it was like having birds singing in his head. He nibbled at it, and his eyes flew wide open as the sugar raced through his body. This, *this*, felt like fireworks! Saliva flooded his mouth, turning the food to a heavenly mud that coated his palate. He smacked his lips, and before he could even think what was the right thing to do next, he shoved the whole lot in his mouth.

He was so giddy with the sugar rush that he staggered, rather than walked, over to the little girl's bed. He could hear her snoring softly, so he scampered quickly under her bed, sidestepping the dust bunnies. He hated the feel of them against his bare feet. He licked the last of the sweetness from his lips as he made a mental note to sweep up under the bed.

He frowned into the darkness under the bed, trying to see what the surprise could be. He hoped it was more food, although his belly was full and swollen. He gave it a little pat and cooed at it. Then he spotted something gleaming and white tucked away beneath the head of the bed, right under the sloping eaves.

The brownie didn't like surprises. New things and too much change made him nervous. So he was a little skittish as he approached the white object, ready to run if it turned out to be something nasty. Like a cat. But as he got closer, his mouth dropped open with surprise and his eyes filled with grateful tears. It was a bed, a little white bed, just like the little girl's. It had a curved headboard and footboard, with tiny little posts topped with balls. It was dressed in white sheets with two plump pillows trimmed with lace and a white duvet, fat as a cloud. He snuffled at the air around it and realized it smelt like plastic – she had probably had one of her dolls lying in it. Such a waste when it was the perfect brownie size! He may have to share the attic room with her, but wait until the other brownies heard he had a proper bed, a HUMAN-type bed!

He reached out to touch it and then gave a squeak of dismay when he realized how grubby he was from a day spent sleeping up the chimney. He let himself down the stairs, trotted to the bathroom and peeped round the door. He rolled his eyes. Just as he thought, the bathroom was rather untidy and a little grubby. This could be his job for the night.

The brownie quite liked doing bathrooms. He tied a sponge to each foot with dental floss, sprayed all around him with some cleaning product and spent the next half-hour skating around the floor. He didn't open the lid of the toilet though – *that* was disgusting. He then peered nervously over the rim of the bath. It was every brownie's nightmare to fall into a bath and to be trapped at the bottom like a spider, curled up and shivering, to be discovered by the household in the morning.

After he tidied up, he ran some hot water into the sink and filled it with bubble bath. He eased himself into the hot water and, with bubbles piling up to his nose, quickly washed himself all over with soap. When he was done, he let the water out and quickly cleaned the sink, rubbing it with his finger until he heard the porcelain squeak.

He ran up the stairs, hugging himself with glee, and clung to the shadows at the sides of the attic room before diving under the bed. He snuggled into the doll's bed, pulling the duvet up around his big ears, and sighed with contentment. It was *sooo* much nicer than sleeping in the chimney, and the feel of clean cotton against his skin was delicious. He wriggled round as he got comfortable. It wasn't perfect, but it wasn't bad. He would have to find some more feathers and scraps of soft cloth to make it like his old bed, but it was a good start.

He gave another huge sigh of content, before yawning and drifting off into a deep sleep.

CHAPTER ELEVEN

As dawn was tinting the night grey, the noise woke Maya up again. She started awake with a cry of fear, as she was ripped from her sleep by that banshee screech. Her heart was hammering so hard in her chest that she thought she could see it beating against her pyjama top. She clutched her duvet to her chest and tried to breathe normally. The bare floorboards stretched away for what seemed like miles towards her bedroom door. The thing that made the noise was outside the house, and she didn't want it to hear her moving around. She knew she should lie very still and quiet, but she was also desperate to make a run for it, across the desert of floorboards, down the stairs and into her parents' bedroom, where their big bed would be warm and safe. She could snuggle down with Mummy and cuddle against her, while Daddy went out to look for the monster. He would make it go away. If she ran very, very fast, she could be in their bedroom in thirty seconds.

Carefully, she slid one foot out from under her duvet and was just about to place her bare toes on the cool wooden boards when the monster made that awful screeching noise again. She gave a little yelp of fear and snatched her foot back under the duvet. She cowered against the sloping eaves and screwed her eyes shut, but two cold tears of pure fear still squeezed their way underneath and wet her face.

"Please make it go away," she whispered in the tee-niest, tiniest voice. "Please, please, please make it go away."

The brownie, who had slept the night away in his lovely new bed for the first time in years, woke up and swivelled an ear in the little girl's direction. He wondered what was frightening her so much, and then he heard the fox call, a little muffled shriek from above and the twang of bed springs as she tried to burrow deep into the bed. He rolled his eyes. Didn't she know it was just a fox?

He could hear her crying now. "Please don't let the monster get me," she said, weeping into her pillow. "Please, help me. I know you can hear me."

He sat up in the bed and frowned. He couldn't just leave her – the poor little thing was terrified. But he couldn't talk to her either. Brownies *never* talked to humans. It had been their code for centuries, no one knew why, but *no one broke the rules*. That was that. He gave a little nod, plumped up his pillows and lay back down, pulling his duvet up around his ears. He closed his eyes and tried to drift back to sleep. But the little girl kept crying. If anything, the sound of her crying was getting louder, even though she was muffling her face with her pillow.

He rolled onto his back and glared at the bed above his head. He was never going to be able to go back to sleep now. He sighed and threw the duvet back.

Maya stopped crying as she heard the little pitter-patter of his feet under her bed. One of her books, a hardback about British wildlife, looked as if it just floated up into the air. It wobbled for a moment, steadied and then glided under her bed. She heard the sound of pages being turned, and then the book, flat on its back and open, skidded out from under the other side of her bed. She peeked over the edge of her mattress and saw a slender little hand, covered in a soft, fine down, fingers tipped with bitten, pale nails, emerge from beneath her bed and tap one of the animals on the page, before shooting back into the darkness.

She leant down and squinted in the dawn gloom at the animal the creature had been pointing at. "It's a fox?" she whispered. "That noise is a fox?" It didn't answer her, but she felt the fear drain out of her, and her body unclenched. She liked foxes. She liked their gingery coats, their long noses and their big, bushy tails. She listened to the sound of them barking, wondering what they were saying to each other as they called across the fields before trotting home to their burrows and their families. She snuggled down into her warm bed, her arms and legs soft and heavy now that the fear had left them. Her eyelids grew heavier, her breathing grew deeper and, before she knew it, she was fast asleep again.

The brownie listened to her sleeping and then crept out from under the bed and peered into her face. Her eyes snapped open, and he held his breath, waiting for her to scream or, even worse, try to talk to him. But she didn't seem to see him at all, and her bright, green eyes glittered like jewels as the first rays of the sun crept into the room. The solitary creature had never looked into another's eyes before, and he stood in the sparkle of her gaze, breathless, until the lids of her eyes closed again and the curl of her eyelashes settled against her smooth cheek. He waited to see her eyes again, but as she slept on, he reached up and gently patted her face, before creeping back to his own warm bed.

CHAPTER TWELVE

Now that she knew she wasn't on her own, Maya slept better at night. If a strange noise woke her up, the creature who slept under her bed used her book to tell her what it was. She didn't know squirrels barked! Best of all, the creature could mimic every sound it heard. They played a game one night, in which Maya pointed at all the animals and birds in her book on British wildlife and the creature imitated barks, hoots, howls and whistles, tucked away in the dark beneath her bed. She was learning to pick out the different birds that lived in the trees and the hedgerows around the house, and her favourite sound was the liquid, tumbling trill of the blackbird. The creature in her room sometimes sang her to sleep with blackbird song. No matter how often she told it to stop, it still waited until they were all asleep at night before working around the house. Of course, Maya got the credit for it, but after a while Mum and Dad stopped asking her about it. Especially as they couldn't catch her doing it. Mum was even relaxing about food. There were chips in the freezer and white bread in the bread bin, and one day she even brought home doughnuts. Maya suspected that Mum was finding all that healthy eating all the time as dull as everyone else. They were all enjoying Mum cooking different stuff, and Maya was beginning to prefer brown rice to white, but it was nice to eat something that felt a bit naughty every now and then. As the summer wore on into the hot, still days of August, Maya was almost beginning to feel at home. School still loomed in September – a big, black cloud squatting on the blue sky of Maya's thoughts – but she tried to ignore it as best she could.

Everything was going so well. Until Liam ruined everything.

Maya had been lying on her stomach on the living-room rug, reading a book. Dad was in his favourite chair, asleep behind his newspaper. Mum was sitting at a small table by the window, carefully framing some pictures to hang on the walls, when they heard Liam yell.

Mum and Maya had looked up at the ceiling in surprise. It sounded as if the yell had come from the attic. The cottage shook and pictures trembled on the walls as Liam thundered down the stairs and burst into the living room, holding up his right hand, which was dripping blood.

"It bit me!" he said, his face as white as chalk. "That thing in her room, IT BIT ME!"

Maya jumped to her feet and yelled "What were you doing in my room?!" as Mum rushed over to Liam with a cry and Dad woke up, thrashing his way through the newspaper to reach the surface.

"Waz goin' on?" asked Dad, bleary-eyed from his afternoon nap.

White-faced, Mum held up Liam's hand. Though blood still welled and trickled down his arm, a neat little semicircle of bite marks could clearly be seen. They all turned to look at Maya.

"I *told* you there was something in my room," she said. She looked at Liam. "What did you do to him?"

"I thought I had left something up in Maya's room…" Liam stammered.

"LIAR!" yelled Maya.

"Stop it!" said Dad. He looked at Mum. "It must be a rat."

Mum put a hand over her mouth, her eyes as wide as saucers. "Think of the diseases it could be carrying," she said. "I'll have to take Liam to the doctor's – that bite could be infected."

Now Liam went white. "Am I going to get rabies?"

"There's no rabies in this country," said Dad. "You'll be OK."

"'Cept you got bitten by a fairy," said Maya. "They might have rabies."

69

"Maya, I mean it, that's ENOUGH!" said Dad, as Liam went green and looked as if he was about to puke.

Mum came running back into the room, her car keys dangling from her fingers. "We've got to go now, Liam. I am going to take you to the hospital," she said, while Dad reached into one of the many unpacked boxes that still lay scattered around the living room and pulled out a tennis racket.

"What are you going to do with that?" asked Maya. "You hate tennis." She felt her tummy prickle with fear as Dad simply strode out of the room, a grim look on his face, not bothering to answer her.

She trotted out after him, dimly aware of the front door slamming as Mum and Liam left for the hospital. She ran up the stairs after her father and gasped when she saw him heading for her room.

"I didn't mean it when I said the fairy had rabies!" she cried as she ran up the attic stairs after him. "Please don't do anything to it!"

Dad still didn't say anything, and Maya was breathless with fear when she caught up with him in the attic. He stood in the middle of her room, glaring around him.

"Where is it?" he asked.

"Daddy, please…"

"Where IS IT, Maya?"

Numb with misery and fear, Maya pointed to her bed. Her father looked at her quickly and then bent down and swiped the tennis racket backwards and forwards beneath her mattress. Maya held her breath, but she didn't hear a squeak of pain and fear. Her father got down on his hands and knees and peered cautiously under the bed. He reached under and pulled out the doll's bed. The sheets were rumpled now with use, and the little creature had been filling it with coloured stones and soft, downy feathers, which fluttered in the breeze her father created as he snatched up the bed.

"Something has been sleeping on this!" said her father, horrified.

"Daddy, I *told* you—"

"Don't tell me any more stories about an invisible friend, Maya – *they don't exist*," said Dad. Maya began to cry as her father shouted at her. "What you've been hearing up here is a rat, Maya – that pitter-pattering you have been talking about, that's the sound their paws make when they scurry around."

"It's not a rat," sobbed Maya.

"What is it then?" asked Dad.

"I don't know," said Maya through her tears. "But it sings me to sleep and tells me what all the noises are at night so that I'm not scared any more. And it's been helping you and Mum with the housework."

Dad sighed. "You've been doing that, Maya, admit it."

"I haven't!" said Maya. "The creature does it, because this is its home and it just wants to be useful. It does

all the work, and all it wants is a tiny bit of porridge."
Too late, Maya realized she shouldn't have said that.

"What do you mean 'it only wants a tiny bit of porridge'?" asked Dad, his voice icy with anger. "Have you
been feeding it, Maya? All the time you've been eating
breakfast in your room, have you been feeding a rat?"

Maya knew that, whatever she said now, Dad wasn't
going to listen, so she just cried harder and louder,
while Dad sat on the floor with a bump and pulled
shaking fingers through his hair. "All this time you've
been telling us about something running around your
room," he said, but he was really talking to himself, not
Maya. "We should have listened. It could have bitten
you in the face when you slept, or something like that."

"It wouldn't do that," sobbed Maya. She jumped
when her father hit the floorboards hard with the flat
of his hand.

"It's vermin, Maya! It's vicious! It's *not* your friend!"
shouted Dad. "We should have believed you when you
told us about it the first time. I'm sorry we didn't take
you seriously, squid. But I would have thought you
would have had more sense than to feed it."

Dad sighed as Maya continued to cry. "You can sleep
with your mother tonight until I get this sorted."

"What are you going to do?" Maya hiccupped.

"I'm going to make sure you are the only one living
in this room," said Dad.

CHAPTER THIRTEEN

Tucked away again on the cold, hard, dirty niche in the chimney, the little brownie trembled with fear and shock. He hadn't meant to bite the horrible boy. He had been tucked up in his bed, fast asleep, as he always was during the day, when that big hand had come swooping in and knocked him onto the ground. If he had not been half asleep, he would have just retreated back into the eaves, but he was frightened and had just reacted, sinking his sharp little teeth into the boy's hand. The brownie made a face and stuck his tongue out, scraping at it with his little hands. He could still taste the boy's skin, and it was yucky!

He had heard what the man said. He wasn't vermin; he *belonged* in this house, had been here since the roof was first raised. He wasn't going anywhere, and brownies were not afraid to fight.

He cocked an ear towards the hearth and listened. The little girl was gone. The room was already cold and empty without her. He felt a little pang in his heart for her, the first person he had communicated with in his long life, the first friend he had ever had. He wondered if she would still be his friend after tonight. But the brownie had to do something. He had nowhere else to go.

He let himself down the chimney and clamped his nose shut with his fingers. The room was full of rat poison, its vile, acid stench singeing the hairs inside his nose. As he breathed through his mouth, he could feel the fumes creeping their way into his mouth, leaving a foul taste on his tongue and making his head buzz. The brownie scurried across the room, carefully avoiding the vicious traps that lay scattered around, their back-breaking metal springs tense and waiting to jump at his lightest footfall. He pulled a pillowcase off one of the pillows, releasing a puff of her warm, milk-and-sugar scent as he did so, which made his stomach clench with grief.

He should have gone straight out – of course he should have – but he missed her. So he crept carefully into the parents' room so he could look at her sleeping face. She was frowning in the moonlight, tucked into her mother's side. Her face was crumpled and he could smell the salt that coated her skin where her tears had dried. Anxiously, he patted a sweaty curl and smoothed sleep-damp hair back from her forehead. She murmured in her sleep, and a tiny little sob escaped her lips. The brownie felt his eyes fill with tears, and he bit his lip hard and clenched his hands into fists. This was why brownies didn't make friends. It hurt far too much.

He pattered down the stairs, dragging the pillowcase in his wake, stopping only to stick his tongue out at the man sleeping on the sofa in the living room. He opened the back door and hesitated for a moment, the doormat's bristles digging painfully into his bare feet. He shivered in the cool night air, terrified of venturing outside.

Brownies rarely went out of the house. The world was very big, and they were very small. There were foxes and weasels and cats lurking in the hedgerows, there were owls and hawks hunting in the sky. Going outside was something a brownie did not do lightly. When he had taken the loud, smelly boy's things outside, he had been desperate, and had thought that one big dramatic act would be enough to secure him a bit of peace and quiet in the house for another fifty years. He whimpered. A brownie shouldn't be outside at all, but twice in one week was torture. But he was desperate. He had to make them understand. And if he couldn't make them understand, he at least had to make them leave him in peace.

He folded the empty pillowcase over and over and tucked the bundle under one arm. He took a deep breath and plunged out into the dark, keeping his body bent at the waist as he ran for the bushes and their inky shadows. He breathed through his mouth in terrified gulps, his ears swivelling to catch every sound in the night. He combed through the dead leaves piled in dry, crackly drifts beneath the hedge with his long fingers. He picked his way through the soft grass and moss of the lawn, every blade wet with dew until he himself was soaked and shivering. Every time he felt what he was looking for, he grabbed at it and dropped it quickly into the pillowcase.

When he thought he had enough, he dragged the now bulging, wriggling pillowcase back into the house, sweat pouring off him as his little arms ached with the strain. The skin on his back crawled as he waited for teeth or talons to punch through his body and swoop him up into a wide, hungry mouth. He was almost crying with fear by the time he reached the doorstep. As soon as he crawled into the safety of the house, he collapsed in relief on the cool flagstone floors, keeping the top of the pillowcase firmly closed with one hand. He panted with relief. He *never* wanted to have to go outside again, *ever*.

He waited until he got his breath back and then climbed to his feet. He gripped the pillowcase in both hands and dragged it alongside him as he made his way to the stairs.

This had better work.

CHAPTER FOURTEEN

Liam's screams woke everyone up early the next morning. Mum leapt up out of the bed and over Maya's sleeping body so fast that Maya nearly tumbled to the floor in her surprise.

"I'm coming, I'm coming," Mum yelled as she dashed across the narrow hallway into Liam's room. Maya heard her shriek as she untangled herself from the bedsheets. As soon as she was free, she padded, barefoot, after her mother. But once she stepped on the first slug and felt it burst against her bare skin like an overripe banana, she regretted not stopping for slippers.

There were slugs everywhere. They were climbing all over the walls, slithering all over the floors; they were in Liam's bed; they were even stuck in his hair. Maya gagged as she hopped on one foot, looking around the room for something she could wipe her skin with. Mum was standing stock-still, white as a sheet, her chest heaving as she tried not to be sick. Mum hated creepy-crawlies of any kind.

"What's going on?!" yelled Dad as he burst into the room, slipped on a handful of unfortunate slugs and fell flat on his back, squishing a few more as he went down. Liam looked at Maya, green and nauseous, and she could swear there were actual tears in his eyes.

"You did this!" he said.

"She couldn't have done," said Mum in a small, strangled voice as she eyed a slug that was stuck vertically to a picture frame on the wall. Its head was pointed in her direction, and it waved its eyes at her. "She's been sleeping in the bed with me all night. She hasn't moved."

Dad climbed, shaking, to his feet, slug guts sprayed like snot to the back of his T-shirt. He looked down and curled his bare toes under as a slug inched its way past.

"How did they all get in here?" he asked.

"She did it to get me back for being in her room yesterday, for messing about with that stupid doll's bed," said Liam, climbing to his feet and trying to stand on a slug-free patch of sheet.

"I told you, Liam: she couldn't have," said Mum, who was beginning to back away to the open door. "I slept with her all night – I was between her and the door. She couldn't have got up without me noticing."

"So who else did it?!" shrieked Liam, as one of the slugs in his hair wandered out too far and slid down his face.

"You know who did it," said Maya in a quiet voice. "It was my friend." She looked at her father. "You've both upset him. If you had just left him alone, he would never have done something like this."

"Maya, I keep telling you: it's just a rat in your room," said Dad.

"I don't think a rat did this," said Maya.

"There has to be a reasonable explanation for how all these slugs got into this room," said Dad. "Why over a thousand slugs decided to pick this one room in the whole house, up a flight of stairs." Maya could hear the disbelief in his voice as he looked around the room.

"Let me know when you find out what it is," said Mum, backing out the open door and bolting for the stairs.

"Hey, who is going to clean this mess up?" yelled Dad.

"I think this counts as one of your jobs," Mum called up the stairs. "I'll get yourself and Liam some gloves, shall I?"

"That's very good of you," called Dad. He didn't try very hard to keep the sarcasm from his voice.

Maya stood there in awkward silence, still balancing on one foot as Dad and Liam looked at her. Well, Liam was really glaring at her, as he turned a darker shade of green. She shrugged. "We should have left him alone," was all she could think of saying as she hopped her way towards the bathroom.

* * *

Mum was making tea when Maya went down to the kitchen. Maya got herself a glass and sat down at the table with her mother and poured herself some milk. She noticed that her mother's hands were shaking as she lifted the cup to her lips.

"Tell me all about this little friend of yours," she whispered.

So Maya told her about the cleaning and the doll's bowls of porridge that were always licked clean, and the way the little creature soothed her to sleep every night with blackbird song – although she decided not to mention anything about the chocolate that Aunt Cass had given her. A few bars were still hidden inside her rucksack.

"Do you really think this friend of yours caught all those slugs and released them into Liam's room?" asked Mum.

Maya nodded, her face solemn. "I do. Liam's been a bit mean to me, and he has been dying to get my room. My friend doesn't want him to move in, because Liam won't leave him any food and he smells."

"Maya, that is a horrible thing to say about your brother!" said Mum.

"'S true though," Maya muttered into her milk.

"So what can we do to make him happy?" Mum asked.

Maya shrugged. "Just leave him alone, I guess," she said. "Just let him do what he has always done. Let

CHAPTER FOURTEEN

him do a bit of cleaning and leave a bit of porridge out for him at night as a reward, and I think he's happy."

Mum sighed. "I can't believe I'm having this conversation."

"I can't believe Liam's room is full of slugs," said Maya.

Mum shuddered. "Please don't remind me. I'm going to have to scrub that room with hot water and bleach."

"I think my friend would like his bed back too," said Maya. "He really liked it."

"I put it in the bin," said Mum. "But don't worry, I'll go into town today and get him a new one – he will have it by bedtime," she quickly added, when she saw how upset Maya was.

"Can you get some more raisins?" asked Maya. "I think he really likes raisins in his porridge. He likes sweet things."

Mum took a deep, shuddering breath. "Look, Maya, let me be honest with you. I'm a grown-up – I don't really believe all this invisible-friend stuff, or that there is a fairy living here willing to do all the housework for a bowl of porridge."

Maya smiled at her sadly and patted her arm. "I know – never mind."

"But there is a lot of stuff that has been going on around here ever since we moved in that I can't explain," Mum continued. "I don't really want to think about it any more, but I would like stuff like slug invasions

81

not to happen. I don't think I could cope if that was to happen on a regular basis. I think I could stand to have the odd bit of housework done and not ask too many questions about who does it. Like I said, I don't want to think about it, and I certainly don't want to talk about it. But you seem to be able to manage all these strange things well enough, so I am going to leave it up to you to make sure things do not get too crazy around here. I'll make sure that whatever needs to be done to keep life simple is done."

Maya nodded.

Mum smiled. "Good. And, like I said, I *never* want to talk about this again."

"Sure," said Maya, taking a sip of her milk.

CHAPTER FIFTEEN

Maya got dressed quickly, and she and Mum left to go into town and get a new bed for the little creature. Mum left strict instructions with Liam and Dad for the cleaning of Liam's room, and then they both ran down the lane to catch the bus into town, laughing as they raced each other. Maya could have hugged her mother in the shop when she described the doll bed they were looking for, just like the one that had been thrown away, and asked the shopkeeper if she would mind checking the stockroom for that exact bed, as she couldn't see it on the shelves, and then spent ages picking the softest, thickest bedding for it so her little friend could be comfortable. Maya could see she was beginning to believe in the little creature, just a little. As soon as they got home, Maya went into the garden and looked for soft, downy bird feathers and pretty coloured stones. She put the new bed in the same spot as the old one and left the feathers and stones around it as a peace offering. Just before bed, Mum made up a small bowl of porridge and studded it with gleaming sultanas, silently handing it to Maya with a faint smile.

Maya left the porridge on the hearth in her room just before dinner. "Everything is going to be OK now," she whispered. "No one is going to bother you any more, and Mum is going to make you food every day."

She listened for a moment, but there wasn't the smallest sound coming from the chimney. She twisted her fingers nervously. She hoped the little creature wasn't angry at her for everything that had happened. None of it had been her fault, but she decided to play it safe, just in case.

"I'm sorry," she said. But still, no answer came.

She sighed and went downstairs for her own dinner. She helped Mum load the dishwasher and got a kiss on the top of her head as a reward. She cuddled up on the sofa with Dad for a while and watched TV until bedtime. When she went back to her room, her heart lifted a little to see the bowl had been licked clean. Maya got ready for bed and brushed her teeth, skipped downstairs to the living room, kissed her parents goodnight and climbed the stairs to her own room.

As she snuggled down into her bed, the duvet pulled up around her ears, she thought of the new doll's bed hidden away beneath her own. She really hoped the little creature was still here, and that by tomorrow night the little bed would be rumpled and creased. She listened to the now familiar sounds of the countryside, as the night predators woke up and went about their business and the night breeze sighed through the treetops. Somewhere a fox barked its wheezy bark. Maya smiled at the sound as her eyelids grew heavier and she drifted off to sleep.

* * *

Some time in the night, that familiar pitter-pattering of little bare feet woke her up, just in time for her to see the little creature trotting away from underneath her bed. He must have climbed down from the chimney and slipped into his new bed while she slept.

"Hey!" she whispered.

The little creature flinched and turned to face her. He was no more than six inches tall, covered in a soft, fine fur like a hamster. He had large ears that swivelled like a dog's to catch every sound, a human-like face and a little pot belly. His eyes were a dark brown, ringed with turquoise, and he wrung his long fingers with anxiety. He looked very, very nervous.

"Did you get enough to eat?" Maya asked. He looked surprised, and then his mouth twitched upwards in the tiniest little smile. He nodded and edged back towards her, pointing at the rucksack.

"You want some chocolate?" asked Maya. The little creature nodded eagerly. "Well, OK, but I can only give you a little bit, because I have to make it last. Are you going to do some cleaning now?" He nodded. "Just do a tiny, teeny bit, because if you do a lot, Mum will have a meltdown." He frowned at her and tipped his head to one side. "Trust me on this," said Maya.

He sighed and shrugged. Then he took a nervous step towards Maya and opened his mouth wide.

"What?" asked Maya, totally confused. "What do you want?"

The little creature continued to point at his open mouth, and Maya realized it was just like the dentist asking her to open her mouth. She leant down out of the bed, opened hers and said, "Aaaah."

He stretched a hand up, and before she could realize what he was doing, he pressed a tiny fingertip against her front teeth and rubbed at them. When they squeaked, he gave a satisfied nod.

"I do know how to clean my teeth!" whispered Maya, indignant.

The little creature shrugged and began to trot away from her, towards the gap in the floorboards where the stairs would lead him down into the house. Maya snuggled back under her duvet and watched him go. He was almost at the stairs when she whispered loudly, "Hey!"

He turned to look at her, a frown creasing his face, and lifted an eyebrow at her.

She looked at him for a moment, and then she pulled the duvet away from her mouth and said, "Goodnight."

His frown deepened as he thought for a moment, and then the loveliest, widest smile lit up his whole face. As clear as a tiny bell being rung in the pre-dawn silence of her room, Maya heard her own voice being mimicked perfectly.

"Goodnight."

Photo: Lou Abercrombie

CHE GOLDEN studied creative writing at Bath University. Her popular *Feral Child* trilogy, published by Quercus, blends Irish mythology and fairy tales.